HOOT

A hole-some book of counting!

LiTTLE TiGER

LONDON

Billy Blue wakes in his nest and finds himself alone. Where have all the others gone?

And why have they all flown?

He dresses in his favourite shirt
(he's always number **one!**)

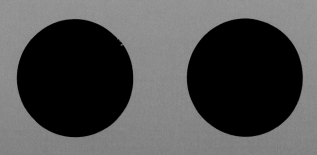

and flies to find his feathered friends
for noisy night-time fun.

From tree to tree he flaps and glides
then shouts a loud

TWIT-TWOO!

"Gertie Green —
you have been seen,
and you plus me
makes two!"

Billy zooms right off again
to see what he can see.
"It's Rodney Red!"
he proudly says —

"Our wide-eyed number three!"

Behind the leaves he thinks he sees
some rustling –
yes, he's sure!

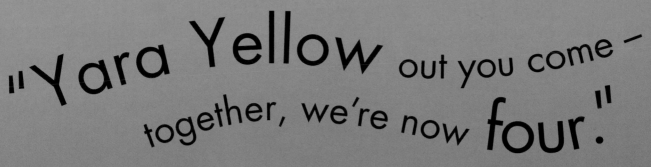

"Yara Yellow out you come – together, we're now four."

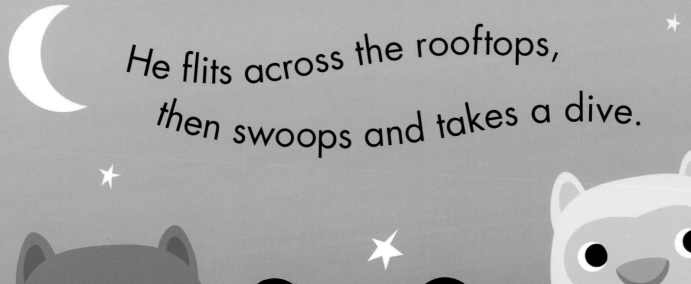

He flits across the rooftops,
then swoops and takes a dive.

"Polly Purple – hide no more!
We're now a gang of **five!**"

Billy says to all the owls,
"I've found you, everyone!
Now close your eyes and count to five –
my hiding turn's begun."

The **other** owls look...

...here...

and there.

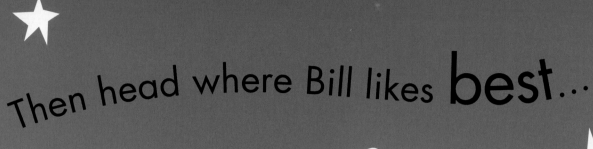

Then head where Bill likes best...

Finally, they find their friend,

snuggled in his nest!